MORE SPECIAL OF
FOR MR MEN AND LITTLE M

KU-519-250

In every Mr Men and Little Miss book like this one, <u>and now</u> in the Mr Men
sticker and activity books, you will find a special token. Collect six tokens and we
will send you a gift of your choice
Choose either a <u>Mr Men</u> or <u>Little Miss</u> poster, **or** a Mr Men or Little Miss
double sided full colour bedroom door hanger.

Return this page **with six tokens per gift required** to:

Marketing Dept., MM / LM, World International Ltd.,
PO Box 7, Manchester, M19 2HD

Your name:_____ Age: _____

Address: _____

_____

_____Postcode: _____

Parent / Guardian Name (Please Print)_____

|← 100 mm →|

ENTRANCE FEE
3 SAUSAGES

250 mm

MR. GREEDY

Please tape a 20p coin to your request to cover part post and package cost

I enclose <u>six</u> tokens per gift, and 20p please send me:-

Posters:-	Mr Men Poster ☐	Little Miss Poster ☐
Door Hangers -	Mr Nosey / Muddle ☐	Mr Greedy / Lazy ☐
	Mr Tickle / Grumpy ☐	Mr Slow / Busy ☐
20p	Mr Messy / Quiet ☐	Mr Perfect / Forgetful ☐
	L Miss Fun / Late ☐	L Miss Helpful / Tidy ☐
	L Miss Busy / Brainy ☐	L Miss Star / Fun ☐

Stick 20p here please

Please Tick Appropriate Box

Collect six of these tokens
You will find one inside every
Mr Men and Little Miss book
which has this special offer.

**1
TOKEN**

We may occasionally wish to advise you of other Mr Men gifts.
If you would rather we didn't please tick this box ☐

Offer open to residents of UK, Channel Isles and Ireland only

Mr Men and Little Miss Library Presentation Boxes

In response to the many thousands of requests for the above, we are delighted to advise that these are now available direct from ourselves,
for only £4.99 (inc VAT) plus 50p p&p.
The full colour boxes accommodate each complete library. They have an integral carrying handle as well as a neat stay closed fastener.
Please do not send cash in the post. Cheques should be made payable to **World International Ltd. for the sum of £5.49** (inc p&p) per box.

Please note books are not included.

Please return this page with your cheque, stating below which presentation box you would like, to:-
Mr Men Office, World International
PO Box 7, Manchester, M19 2HD

Your name:_____

Address: _____

_____

_____Postcode: _____

Name of Parent/Guardian (please print):_____

Signature:_____

I enclose a cheque for £_____ made payable to World International Ltd.,

Please send me a Mr Men Presentation Box ☐

Little Miss Presentation Box ☐ (please tick or write in quantity)
and allow 28 days for delivery

Thank you

Offer applies to UK, Eire & Channel Isles only

little Miss Stubborn

by Roger Hargreaves

WORLD INTERNATIONAL

Little Miss Stubborn was, as you might imagine,
extraordinarily stubborn.

Once she had made her mind up
there was no unmaking it.

If she decided to go out,
she went out.

Even when it was pouring with rain!

One Sunday, when it wasn't raining,
she decided to take the bus
to Mr Strong's house.

Why?

Because she had run out of eggs.

And, as everybody knows,
Mr Strong always has lots of eggs.

As the bus arrived, Mr Nosey walked by.

Being nosey, he couldn't help asking:

"Where are you going, Little Miss Stubborn?"

"To Mr Strong's house," she said.

"But this bus doesn't go anywhere near there!"

But Little Miss Stubborn took the bus anyway.

And you won't be surprised to hear it didn't
go anywhere near Mr Strong's house.

It went to Coldland.

A country where it is so cold
that everybody has a cold all year round.

"What a charming place!" she said, shivering
and trying to look as if she had really planned
on coming to Coldland in the first place.

Which of course she hadn't.

As you know.

She ran along a path to keep warm.

"ATISHOO!" somebody sneezed all of a sudden.

It was Mr Sneeze.

"If I were you," he warned, "I wouldn't
take … ATISHOO! that path. It's icy! ATISHOO!"

"I'll take it if I want to!" snorted
Little Miss Stubborn.

And she followed the path.

But can you guess what happened?

WHOOOOOOOSH!

She slipped on the ice!

"That was fun!" said Little Miss Stubborn.

But of course it wasn't.

She came to a fork in the path.

"I shall go this way," she said,
taking the right hand path.

"You're making a big mistake!" said a worm,
popping his head through the snow.
"This way isn't safe."

"Don't be silly!" cried Little Miss Stubborn
and started off down the path.

She should have listened to the worm!

Before she had gone very far
an avalanche of snowballs fell on top of her!

One of the snowballs rolled off the path
and rolled and rolled down a very steep hill.

And, inside it,
Little Miss Stubborn rolled and rolled
down the very steep hill as well.

The snowball rolled a very long way,
all the way into a different country
where it melted.

As luck would have it,
Little Miss Stubborn found herself
outside Mr Strong's front door.

She was soaked to the skin.

"My goodness! You're wet through!"
said Mr Strong.
"Quick, come in and dry yourself
before you catch a cold."

"I don't catch colds," said Little Miss Stubborn.
"Anyway, I've come for some eggs.
Out of my way!"

"That's no way to behave," said Mr Strong.

"Rubbish!" snorted Little Miss Stubborn.

Still wet through,
she marched into Mr Strong's kitchen.

Without a please or a thank you,
she helped herself to a large bowl of eggs.

"You could at least ask," said Mr Strong.

"ATISHOO!" sneezed Little Miss Stubborn.

"I told you you'd catch a cold," said Mr Strong.

"I don't catch colds," said Little Miss Stubborn,
and sneezed again, "ATISHOO!"

She was so hungry by this time
that, there and then, she made herself
an enormous omelette.

It was gigantic.

It was so big that it won't even fit on the page!

Then she began to eat her enormous,
gigantic omelette.

And the more she ate, the more worried
Mr Strong became:
"You'll make yourself ill," he said.

"Fiddlesticks," snorted Little Miss Stubborn,
and because she was who she was,
she finished that enormous, gigantic omelette.

And there is not much more to add.

Other than now you know how
extraordinarily stubborn
Little Miss Stubborn is!

Stubborn to the very end …
the very end of this story.